Paper Bag Trail

Written by Anne Schreiber and Arbo Doughty

Pictures by Ward Schumaker

SCHOLASTIC INC.

New York   Toronto   London   Auckland   Sydney

Copyright © 1994 by Scholastic Inc.
All rights reserved. Published by Scholastic Inc.
Printed in the U.S.A.
ISBN 0-590-27373-6

     6 7 8 9 10   08   00 99 98 97 96

Lee ate some popcorn
and threw the bag away.

The wind picked it up
and blew it away.

The dog picked it up
and took it away.

The ants picked it up
and dragged it away.

8

The bird picked it up
and carried it away.

The rain picked it up
and washed it away.

12

14

Guess what Lee did?
Lee picked it up and
threw it away, again!